"I'm lonely.
I have **no friends**,"
says Bush Baby.

"Will you be my friend?"

SoU

WITHDRAWN

Books should be returned or renewed by the last
date above. Renew by phone **03000 41 31 31** or
online *www.kent.gov.uk/libs*

"No way," says Giraffe.
"You're much **too** small.
I can hardly see you
down there."

"Will you be my friend?"

"Nah. You have a **tail**,"
says Toad.
"I don't understand tails.
Mine vanished when
I was a tadpole.
You should have a
l–o–n–g tongue
instead."

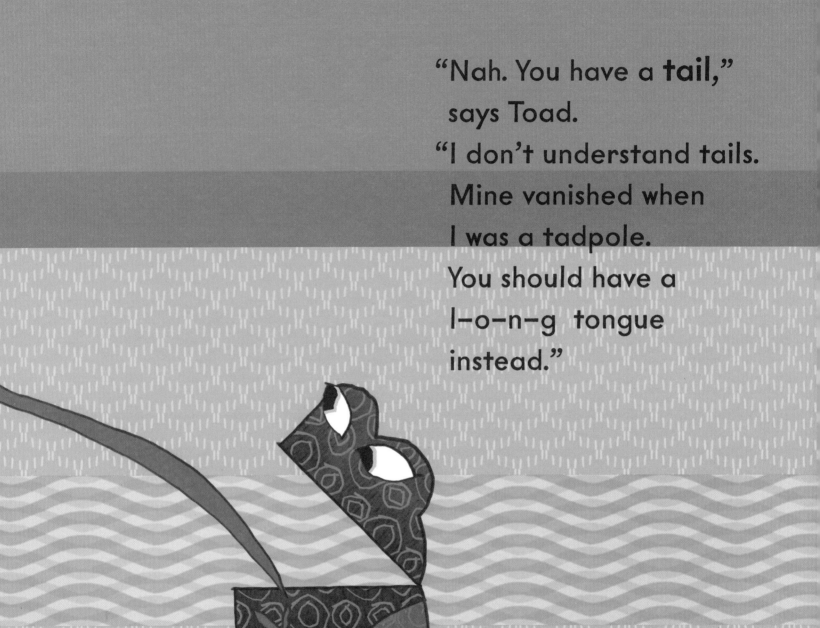

"Will you be my friend?"

"What?" says Zebra.
"I can't be seen with you.

You have **no stripes**.
Where are your stripes?
No stripes won't do."

"Will you be my friend?"

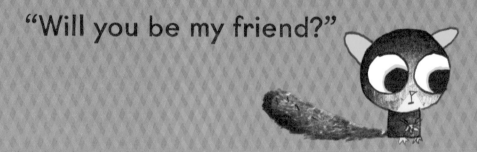

"Don't be ss-silly,"
says Snake.
"You have far **too**
many legs-ss.

See? No legs-ss."

"Will..."

"Absolutely not," says Flamingo.
"Don't even think about it.
You're totally the wrong colour.
PINK is the right colour.
P.I.N.K. PINK!"

"No one wants to be **my friend**.
Nobody even likes me.
Nobody in the whole wide world.
I'll just go away and be on my own...
forever."

"I can't decide,"
says Lion.
"Are you very brave,
or very foolish?"

"I'm **very** lonely,"
says Bush Baby.
"I have no friends.
And nobody wants
to be my friend."

"Oh," says Lion.
"I have no friends either.
Everyone thinks
I might eat them for
some reason.

But I would **never** eat a friend.
That would be **most** unfriendly."

"Will you be...
oh I know,
I look all **wrong**
to be your friend."

"You look all **right** to me," says Lion. "You'll be a **perfect** friend."

Then all the other animals say,
"We'd like to be **your** friends **now**."

Bush Baby says,
"What do you think,
Lion?"

And Lion says,
"I think I'm getting **very...**"